NFL'S GREATEST PLAYERS

QUARTERBACKS

By Tammy Gagne

Kaleidoscope
Minneapolis, MN

Your Front Row Seat to the Games

This edition first published in 2020 by Kaleidoscope Publishing, Inc.

For information regarding permission, write to
Kaleidoscope Publishing, Inc.
6012 Blue Circle Drive
Minnetonka, MN 55343

Library of Congress Control Number
2019939222

ISBN
978-1-64519-076-9 (library bound)
978-1-64494-172-0 (paperback)
978-1-64519-177-3 (ebook)

Printed in the United States of America.

TABLE OF CONTENTS

CHAPTER 1

Tom Brady looks up at the scoreboard in Super Bowl LI.

A Historic Comeback

Tom Brady was not used to losing. The New England Patriots quarterback was his team's star player. He looked up at the Super Bowl LI scoreboard. It was a sad sight. The Patriots were losing to the Atlanta Falcons 28–3. Brady had been to six Super Bowls. But he had never faced anything like this. Brady did not have time to feel bad. It was late in the third quarter. He had to get to work.

The Patriots faced fourth down. They had to go for it. Brady dropped back. He found **wide receiver** Danny Amendola. The catch went for a first down.

Brady later faced third and eight. He looked around. Nobody was open. He took off running. He got the first down. Then he finished the drive. He threw to **running back** James White. Touchdown!

Brady was on fire. The Falcons could not stop him. He threw for another score. It went to Amendola again.

FUN FACT

Brady was the first Patriots quarterback to win a Super Bowl.

That made the score 28–20. Then White scored again. It was 28–26. There was less than a minute left. The Patriots had to go for two points. Brady took the snap. He fired a quick pass to Amendola. He caught it! New England tied the game at 28.

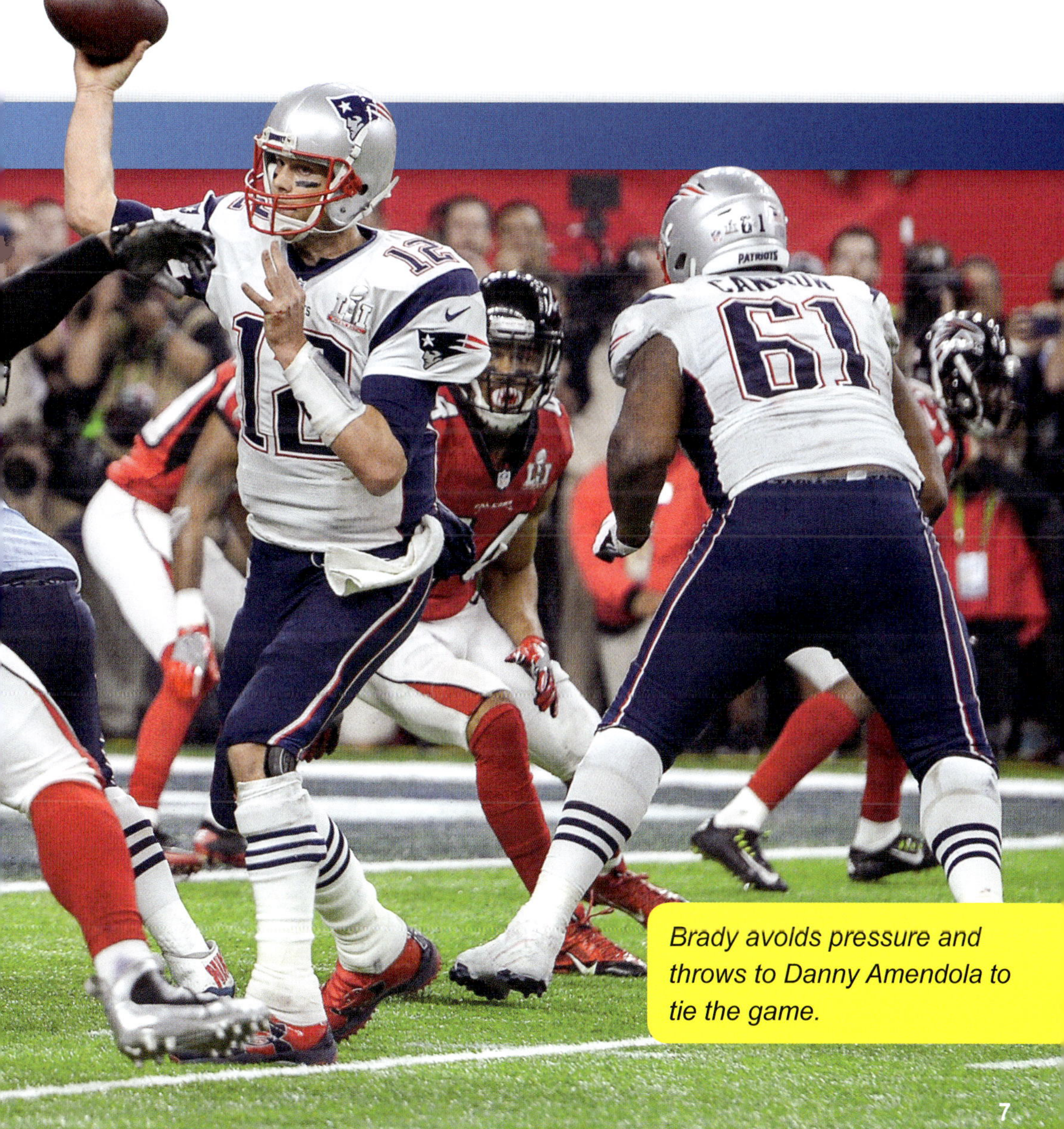

Brady avoids pressure and throws to Danny Amendola to tie the game.

Brady celebrates with the Super Bowl LI trophy after leading the comeback win.

The Falcons could not believe it. The Patriots had forced overtime. And Brady could not be stopped there, either. He completed five passes in a row. Then White ran in his third score. The whistle blew. The game was over. The final score was 34–28.

The Patriots erased a 25-point **deficit** to win. It was the biggest comeback in Super Bowl history. And Brady made it happen. He was named the game's Most Valuable Player (MVP).

SMASHING RECORDS

The old record for largest Super Bowl comeback was ten points. Brady did not only break that record. He also broke his own record. He had once made a comeback from twenty-four points. Now his record was twenty-five.

CHAPTER 2

Aaron Rodgers throws on the run in a 2018 game against Atlanta.

What Makes a Successful QB?

Aaron Rodgers dropped back. He threw a pass into the air. It was heading for wide receiver Randall Cobb. It flew 24 yards. The pass was right on target. Cobb easily caught it in the end zone. Touchdown! Rodgers made a lot of these throws for the Green Bay Packers. But this one was a record. It was his 359th pass in a row without an **interception**. The Packers beat the Falcons 30–20.

Football teams are made up of three position groups. One is defense. They try to stop the other team. There is also special teams. They kick and punt. Then there is the offense. They try to move the ball down the field. And the QB leads the offense.

FUN FACT

Rodgers has thrown ten or more interceptions only twice: in 2008 and 2010.

Many people consider the quarterback the most important player. He makes decisions on the field. He talks to his teammates in the **huddle**. He tells them which plays they will run. The decisions he makes can decide the winner of a game.

Rodgers is one of the best QBs in the National Football League (NFL). He has all the skills that make a good QB. He has a strong arm. He can throw the ball on target. Those two things make any throw possible.

The best QBs also are smart. They have to think quickly. They must know the plays. They have to make sure everyone knows the plays.

WHERE QUARTERBACKS LINE UP

The quarterback's position at the start of a play is directly behind the offensive line.

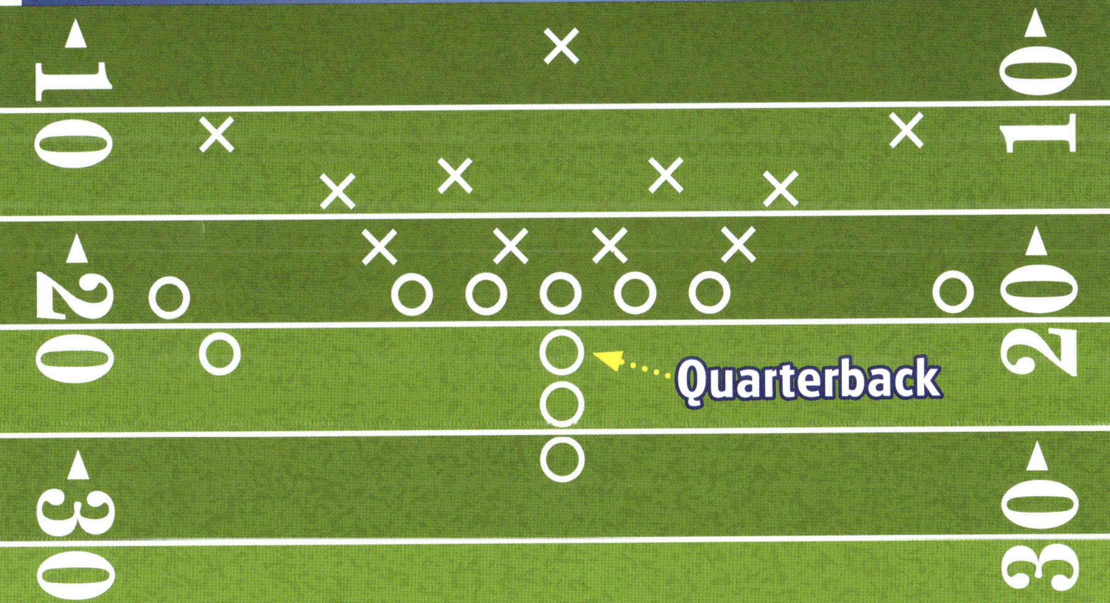

Quarterbacks like Rodgers and Tom Brady do not panic when things go wrong. Brady's Patriots had the lead in a 2018 game. They were playing the Kansas City Chiefs. Chiefs receiver Tyreek Hill was heading toward the end zone with the ball. His touchdown tied the score. There were just three minutes left.

Quarterbacks such as the Chicago Bears' Mitchell Trubisky (10) talk over plays with their teammates in the huddle.

Many Patriots fans were worried. But Brady smiled. He was ready to go back in. He had great **concentration**. He led a scoring drive to win the game.

CHAPTER 3

The Greatest to Play the Game

Joe Montana was calm under pressure. Fans called him "Joe Cool." Montana led the San Francisco 49ers to Super Bowl XVI. It was his first time playing in the big game. It did not look like it. Montana ran for a score. He later led a 92-yard touchdown drive. That was the longest in Super Bowl history. By halftime the 49ers led 20–0. Montana was named the game MVP. His team won 26–21.

FUN FACT

Montana did not throw a single interception in four Super Bowls.

Joe Montana drops back to pass in Super Bowl XVI.

John Elway (7) runs away from pressure in a 1987 game against the Cleveland Browns.

There have been many great quarterbacks. But few are the same. Roger Staubach played for the Dallas Cowboys. He was known for **improvising**. Sometimes his first plan failed. But Staubach figured out a way to make the play.

The most exciting football games often have surprise endings. Denver Broncos quarterback John Elway played in a lot of those. Elway was known for comeback wins. One was called "The Drive." It happened in 1987. Elway led a 98-yard touchdown drive. The Broncos tied the score with 37 seconds left. They then beat the Cleveland Browns in overtime. Denver went on to the Super Bowl.

Roger Staubach

TIMELINE OF TOP QUARTERBACKS

1965

Roger Staubach,
Dallas Cowboys
(1969–79)

1975

Joe Montana,
San Francisco 49ers
(1979–92),
Kansas City Chiefs
(1993–94)

John Elway,
Denver Broncos
(1983–98)

1985

Troy Aikman,
Dallas Cowboys
(1989–2000)

1995

Peyton Manning,
Indianapolis Colts
(1998–2010),
Denver Broncos
(2012–15)

Tom Brady,
New England Patriots
(2000–)

Drew Brees,
San Diego Chargers
(2001–05),
New Orleans Saints
(2006–)

2005

Aaron Rodgers,
Green Bay Packers
(2005–)

Russell Wilson,
Seattle Seahawks
(2012–)

2015

Troy Aikman was another great QB for the Cowboys. He was known for his strength. His high school coach nicknamed him "Iceman." He was cool on the field.

QBs must have a plan. Peyton Manning knew this. He spent lots of time preparing for games. He would practice late into the night. He often slept at the stadium. He stayed up late watching film of the other team. His hard work paid off. Manning played in four Super Bowls. He won one with the Indianapolis Colts and one with the Denver Broncos.

Peyton Manning, left, studies some information on the sideline during a 2014 game.

CHAPTER 4

The Next All-Time Greats

Patrick Mahomes played his first NFL game in 2017. But he showed quickly he could be an all-time great. He led the Kansas City Chiefs to a division title in 2018. He threw for 50 touchdowns. His first one was special. It came in a game against the Los Angeles Chargers. He threw a 58-yard bomb to Tyreek Hill. Kansas City won 38–28.

Baker Mayfield earns respect. The Cleveland Browns QB keeps cool in tough spots. Mayfield hit the field with less than two minutes left in a 2018 game. The New York Jets knew he was a **rookie**. One player tried to distract him with trash talk.

Patrick Mahomes

PATRICK MAHOMES

IN 2018

LONGEST PASS	89 YARDS
INTERCEPTIONS	12
PASSING YARDS	5,097
PASSING TOUCHDOWNS	50
PASSER RATING	113.8

But Mayfield did not let it get to him. He looked the other player straight in the eye. Mayfield told him he didn't even know who he was. Seconds later Mayfield threw a 14-yard pass.

Confidence helps quarterbacks succeed after failing. Cam Newton lost eight of the first ten games he played for the Carolina Panthers in 2011. But that did not stop him. He stayed positive. He trusted his skills. He led his team to four wins in five games in November and December. By 2015, he was NFL MVP. And he led the Panthers to the Super Bowl.

STILL LEADING THEIR TEAMS

A few current quarterbacks already rank among the all-time great list. Tom Brady, Drew Brees, and Aaron Rodgers have all been playing for many years. Yet they continue to dazzle fans with their impressive plays. Brady has won more Super Bowls than any other quarterback in NFL history.

Baker Mayfield calls out to a teammate before a play in a 2018 game.

FUN FACT
The Eagles won the Super Bowl after the 2017 season, but Wentz was hurt and could not play.

Carson Wentz dives for a touchdown in a 2016 game against Green Bay.

Carson Wentz is a quick thinker on the field. In 2018 he and his Philadelphia Eagles played the Indianapolis Colts. He dove for a first down like a superhero.

When the Colts tried to tackle him, he spun out of the way. When they did hit him, he moved on. He found a way to make plays. These skills could make him another all-time great.

BEYOND THE BOOK

After reading the book, it's time to think about what you learned. Try the following exercises to jumpstart your ideas.

THINK

THAT'S NEWS TO ME. How might news sources offer more information about the plays that helped Tom Brady and the New England Patriots win Super Bowl LI in the fourth quarter of the game? What new information could be found in news articles? Where could you go to find those news sources?

CREATE

SHARPEN YOUR RESEARCH SKILLS. Chapter Two discusses the role of a quarterback. Where could you go in the library or to whom could you talk to find out more about this subject?

SHARE

SUM IT UP. Write one paragraph summarizing the important points from the whole book. Be sure to write this paragraph in your own words. Do not just copy what was in the text. Next, share the paragraph with a classmate. Ask this classmate for feedback or additional questions about the topic after reading your summary.

GROW

REAL-LIFE RESEARCH. Consider real-world places you could visit to do more research about football. For example, could you attend a professional or high school game? Could you watch a football practice at your school or community center? What other topics could also be explored at these events?

Visit www.ninjaresearcher.com/0769 to learn how to take your research skills and book report writing to the next level!

RESEARCH

SEARCH LIKE A PRO
Learn about how to use search engines to find useful websites.

FACT OR FAKE?
Discover how you can tell a trusted website from an untrustworthy resource.

TEXT DETECTIVE
Explore how to zero in on the information you need most.

SHOW YOUR WORK
Research responsibly—learn how to cite sources.

WRITE

GET TO THE POINT
Learn how to express your main ideas.

PLAN OF ATTACK
Learn prewriting exercises and create an outline.

DOWNLOADABLE REPORT FORMS

Further Resources

BOOKS

Fishman, John M. *Aaron Rodgers*. Lerner Publications, 2019.

Leventhal, Josh. *Quarterbacks*. Black Rabbit Books, 2017.

Uhl, Xina M. *Tom Brady*. Rosen, 2019.

WEBSITES

FACTSURFER

Factsurfer.com gives you a safe, fun way to find more information.

1. Go to www.factsurfer.com.
2. Enter "Quarterbacks" into the search box and click .
3. Select your book cover to see a list of related websites.

Glossary

concentration: Concentration is the ability to focus one's attention. The opposing team's double-digit lead did not break the quarterback's concentration.

deficit: When one team is behind another in points, that difference is a deficit. The Dallas Cowboys narrowed the deficit by six points.

huddle: A huddle is a quick meeting of football players on the field between plays. The quarterback described his strategy to his teammates during the huddle.

improvising: Improvising is making effective decisions despite having little preparation. The quarterback's improvising ability saved his team late in the game.

interception: A pass that is thrown by one team and caught by a player on the opposing team is an interception. The quarterback's final pass ended in an interception.

rookie: A rookie is an athlete in his or her first year in a new league. The crowd cheered as the rookie quarterback scored his first touchdown.

running back: An offensive football player whose main job is carrying the ball down the field is the running back. The running back escaped a tackle by the opposing team.

wide receiver: An offensive football player who receives passes is called a wide receiver. The wide receiver caught the ball the quarterback threw to him.

Index

PHOTO CREDITS

The images in this book are reproduced through the courtesy of: Paul Jasienski/AP Images, front cover (center); Jeff Haynes/Panini/AP Images, front cover (left), p. 3; Michael Ainsworth/AP Images, front cover (right); EFKS/Shutterstock Images, front cover (background); Gregory Payan/AP Images, pp. 4–5; Jeff Bukowski/Shutterstock Images, pp. 5, 9, 16, 20 (top); Anthony Behar/Sipa USA/AP Images, pp. 6–7; Ben Liebenberg/AP Images, p. 8; Matt Ludtke/AP Images, pp. 10–11; Jeffrey Phelps/AP Images, p. 12; Red Line Editorial, pp. 13, 20 (timeline), 23 (chart); Aaron M. Sprecher/AP Images, pp. 14–15; AP Images, pp. 16–17; Gene Pushkar/AP Images, p. 18; Al Messerschmidt/AP Images, p. 19; dean bertoncelj/Shutterstock Images, p. 20 (bottom); Damian Strohmeyer/AP Images, p. 21; Jamie Lamor Thompson/Shutterstock Images, p. 22; Charlie Riedel/AP Images, p. 23; Ron Schwane/AP Images, pp. 24–25; Michael Perez/AP Images, pp. 26–27; Gerald Herbert/AP Images, p. 30.

ABOUT THE AUTHOR

Tammy Gagne has written dozens of books for both adults and children. Her recent titles include *John Cena* and *Dodge Viper SRT*. She lives in northern New England with her husband, son, and a menagerie of pets.